THE OLD DIE RICH

Start Publishing PD is a registered trademark of Start Publishing PD LLC
Manufactured in the United States of America

Cover art: Shutterstock/Taisiya Kozorez

Cover design: Jennifer Do

10 9 8 7 6 5 4 3 2 1

ISBN 979-8-8809-1881-2

THE OLD DIE RICH

by H. L. Gold

It is the kind of news item you read at least a dozen times a year, wonder about briefly, and then promptly forget—but the real story is the one that the reporters are unable to cover!

*

You again, Weldon," the Medical Examiner said wearily.

I nodded pleasantly and looked around the shabby room with a feeling of hopeful eagerness. Maybe *this* time, I thought, I'd get the answer. I had the same sensation I always had in these places—the quavery senile despair at being closed in a room with the single shaky chair, tottering bureau, dim bulb hanging from the ceiling, the flaking metal bed.

There was a woman on the bed, an old woman with white hair thin enough to show the tight-drawn scalp, her face and body so emaciated that the flesh between the bones formed parchment pockets. The M.E. was going over her as if she were a side of beef that he had to put a federal grade stamp on, grumbling meanwhile about me and Sergeant Lou Pape, who had brought me here.

"When are you going to stop taking Weldon around to these cases, Sergeant?" the M.E. demanded in annoyance. "Damned actor and his morbid curiosity!"

For the first time, Lou was stung into defending me. "Mr. Weldon is a friend of mine—I used to be an actor, too, before I joined the force—and he's a follower of Stanislavsky."

The beat cop who'd reported the D.O.A. whipped around at the door. "A Red?"

*

I let Lou Pape explain what the Stanislavsky method of acting was, while I sat down on the one chair and tried to apply it. Stanislavsky was the great pre-Revolution Russian stage director whose idea was that actors had to think and feel like the characters they portrayed so they could *be* them. A Stanislavskian works out everything about a character right up to the point where a play starts—where he was born, when, his relationship with his parents, education, childhood,

4

adolescence, maturity, attitudes toward men, women, sex, money, success, including incidents. The play itself is just an extension of the life history created by the actor.

How does that tie in with the old woman who had died? Well, I'd had the cockeyed kind of luck to go bald at 25 and I'd been playing old men ever since. I had them down pretty well—it's not just a matter of shuffling around all hunched over and talking in a high cracked voice, which is cornball acting, but learning what old people are like inside—and these cases I talked Lou Pape into taking me on were studies in senility. I wanted to understand them, know what made them do what they did, *feel* the compulsion that drove them to it.

The old woman on the bed, for instance, had $32,000 in five bank accounts ... and she'd died of starvation.

You've come across such cases in the news, at least a dozen a year, and wondered who they were and why they did it. But you read the items, thought about them for a little while, and then forgot them. My interest was professional; I made my living playing old people and I had to know as much about them as I could.

That's how it started off, at any rate. But the more cases I investigated, the less sense they made to me, until finally they were practically an obsession.

Look, they almost always have around $30,000 pinned to their underwear, hidden in mattresses, or parked in the bank, yet they starve themselves to death. If I could understand them, I could write a play or have one written; I might really make a name for myself, even get a Hollywood contract, maybe, if I could act them as they should be acted.

So I sat there in the lone chair, trying to reconstruct the character of the old woman who had died rather than spend a single cent of her $32,000 for food.

*

Malnutrition induced by senile psychosis," the M.E. said, writing out the death certificate. He turned to me. "There's no mystery to it, Weldon. They starve because they're less afraid of death than digging into their savings."

I'd been imagining myself growing weak from hunger and trying to decide that I ought to eat even if it cost me something. I came out of it and said, "That's what you keep telling me."

"I keep hoping it'll convince you so you won't come around any more. What are the chances, Weldon?"

"Depends. I will when I'm sure you're right. I'm not."

He shrugged disgustedly, ordered the wicker basket from the meat wagon and had the old woman carried out. He and the beat cop left with the basket team. He could at least have said good-by. He never did, though.

A fat lot I cared about his attitude or dogmatic medical opinion. Getting inside this character was more important. The setting should have helped; it was depressing, rank with the feel of solitary desperation and needless death.

Lou Pape stood looking out the one dirty window, waiting patiently for me. I let my joints stiffen as if they were thirty years older and more worn out than they were, and empathized myself into a dilemma between getting still weaker from hunger and drawing a little money out of the bank.

I worked at it for half an hour or so with the deep concentration you acquire when you use the Stanislavsky method. Then I gave up.

"The M.E. is wrong, Lou," I said. "It doesn't feel right."

Lou turned around from the window. He'd stood there all that time without once coughing or scratching or doing anything else that might have distracted me. "He knows his business, Mark."

"But he doesn't know old people."

"What is it you don't get?" he prompted, helping me dig my way through a characterization like the trained Stanislavskian he was—and still would have been if he hadn't gotten so sick of the insecurity of acting that he'd become a cop. "Can't money be more important to a psychotic than eating?"

"Sure," I agreed. "Up to a point. Undereating, yes. Actual starvation, no."

"Why not?"

"You and the M.E. think it's easy to starve to death. It isn't. Not when you can buy day-old bread at the bakeries, soup bones for about a nickel a pound, wilted vegetables that groceries are glad to get rid of. Anybody who's willing to eat that stuff can stay alive on nearly nothing a day. Nearly nothing, Lou, and hunger is a damned potent instinct. I can understand hating to spend even those few cents. I can't see going without food altogether."

*

He took out a cigarette; he hadn't until then because he didn't want to interrupt my concentration. "Maybe they get too weak to go out after old bread and meat bones and wilted vegetables."

"It still doesn't figure." I got up off the shaky chair, my joints now really stiff from sitting in it. "Do you know how long it takes to die of starvation?"

"That depends on age, health, amount of activity—"

"Nuts!" I said. "It would take weeks!"

"So it takes weeks. Where's the problem—if there is one?"

I lit the pipe I'd learned to smoke instead of cigarettes—old men seem to use pipes more than anything else, though maybe it'll be different in the next generation. More cigarette smokers now, you see, and they'd stick to the habit unless the doctor ordered them to cut it out.

"Did you ever try starving for weeks, Lou?" I asked.

"No. Did you?"

"In a way. All these cases you've been taking me on for the last couple of years—I've tried to be them. But let's say it's possible to die of starvation when you have thousands of dollars put away. Let's say you don't think of scrounging off food stores or working out a way of

7

freeloading or hitting soup lines. Let's say you stay in your room and slowly starve to death."

He slowly picked a fleck of tobacco off his lip and flicked it away, his sharp black eyes poking holes in the situation I'd built up for him. But he wasn't ready to say anything yet.

"There's charity," I went on, "relief—except for those who have their dough in banks, where it can be checked on—old age pension, panhandling, cadging off neighbors."

He said, "We know these cases are hermits. They don't make contact with anybody."

"Even when they're starting to get real hungry?"

"You've got something, Mark, but that's the wrong tack," he said thoughtfully. "The point is that *they* don't have to make contact; other people know them or about them. Somebody would check after a few days or a week—the janitor, the landlord, someone in the house or the neighborhood."

"So they'd be found before they died."

"You'd think so, wouldn't you?" he agreed reluctantly. "They don't generally have friends, and the relatives are usually so distant, they hardly know these old people and whether they're alive or not. Maybe that's what threw us off. But you don't need friends and relatives to start wondering, and investigate when you haven't shown up for a while." He lifted his head and looked at me. "What does that prove, Mark?"

"That there's something wrong with these cases. I want to find out what."

*

I got Lou to take me down to Headquarters, where he let me see the bankbooks the old woman had left.

"She took damned good care of them," I said. "They look almost new."

"Wouldn't you take damned good care of the most important thing in the world to you?" he asked. "You've seen the hoards of money the

8

others leave. Same thing."

I peered closely at the earliest entry, April 23, 1907, $150. My eyes aren't that bad; I was peering at the ink. It was dark, unfaded. I pointed it out to Lou.

"From not being exposed to daylight much," he said. "They don't haul out the bankbooks or money very often, I guess."

"And that adds up for you? I can see them being psychotics all their lives ... but not *senile* psychotics."

"They hoarded, Mark. That adds up for me."

"Funny," I said, watching him maneuver his cigarette as if he loved the feel of it, drawing the smoke down and letting it out in plumes of different shapes, from rings to slender streams. What a living he could make doing cigarette commercials on TV! "I can see *you* turn into one of these cases, Lou."

He looked startled for a second, but then crushed out the butt carefully so he could watch it instead of me. "Yeah? How so?"

"You've been too scared by poverty to take a chance. You know you could do all right acting, but you don't dare giving up this crummy job. Carry that far enough and you try to stop spending money, then cut out eating, and finally wind up dead of starvation in a cheap room."

"Me? I'd never get that scared of being broke!"

"At the age of 70 or 80?"

"Especially then! I'd probably tear loose for a while and then buy into a home for the aged."

I wanted to grin, but I didn't. He'd proved my point. He'd also shown that he was as bothered by these old people as I was.

"Tell me, Lou. If somebody kept you from dying, would you give him any dough for it, even if you were a senile psychotic?"

I could see him using the Stanislavsky method to feel his way to the answer. He shook his head. "Not while I was alive. Will it, maybe, not give it."

"How would that be as a motive?"

*

He leaned against a metal filing cabinet. "No good, Mark. You know what a hell of a time we have tracking down relatives to give the money to, because these people don't leave wills. The few relatives we find are always surprised when they get their inheritance—most of them hardly remember dear old who-ever-it-was that died and left it to them. All the other estates eventually go to the State treasury, unclaimed."

"Well, it was an idea." I opened the oldest bankbook again. "Anybody ever think of testing the ink, Lou?"

"What for? The banks' records always check. These aren't forgeries, if that's what you're thinking."

"I don't know what I'm thinking," I admitted. "But I'd like to turn a chemist loose on this for a little while."

"Look, Mark, there's a lot I'm willing to do for you, and I think I've done plenty, but there's a limit—"

I let him explain why he couldn't let me borrow the book and then waited while he figured out how it could be done and did it. He was still grumbling when he helped me pick a chemist out of the telephone directory and went along to the lab with me.

"But don't get any wrong notions," he said on the way. "I have to protect State property, that's all, because I signed for it and I'm responsible."

"Sure, sure," I agreed, to humor him. "If you're not curious, why not just wait outside for me?"

He gave me one of those white-tooth grins that he had no right to deprive women audiences of. "I could do that, but I'd rather see you make a sap of yourself."

I turned the bankbook over to the chemist and we waited for the report. When it came, it had to be translated.

*

The ink was typical of those used 50 years ago. Lou Pape gave me a jab in the ribs at that. But then the chemist said that, according to the amount of oxidation, it seemed fresh enough to be only a few months or years old, and it was Lou's turn to get jabbed. Lou pushed him about the aging, asking if it couldn't be the result of unusually good care. The chemist couldn't say—that depended on the kind of care; an airtight compartment, perhaps, filled with one of the inert gases, or a vacuum. They hadn't been kept that way, of course, so Lou looked as baffled as I felt.

He took the bankbook and we went out to the street.

"See what I mean?" I asked quietly, not wanting to rub it in.

"I see something, but I don't know what. Do you?"

"I wish I could say yes. It doesn't make any more sense than anything else about these cases."

"What do you do next?"

"Damned if I know. There are thousands of old people in the city. Only a few of them take this way out. I have to try to find them before they do."

"If they're loaded, they won't say so, Mark, and there's no way of telling them from those who are down and out."

I rubbed my pipe disgruntledly against the side of my nose to oil it. "Ain't this a beaut of a problem? I wish I liked problems. I hate them."

Lou had to get back on duty. I had nowhere to go and nothing to do except worry my way through this tangle. He headed back to Headquarters and I went over to the park and sat in the sun, warming myself and trying to think like a senile psychotic who would rather die of starvation than spend a few cents for food.

I didn't get anywhere, naturally. There are too many ways of beating starvation, too many chances of being found before it's too late.

And the fresh ink, over half a century old....

*

I took to hanging around banks, hoping I'd see someone come in with an old bankbook that had fresh ink from 50 years before. Lou was some help there—he convinced the guards and tellers that I wasn't an old-looking guy casing the place for a gang, and even got the tellers to watch out for particularly dark ink in ancient bankbooks.

I stuck at it for a month, although there were a few stage calls that didn't turn out right, and one radio and two TV parts, which did and kept me going. I was almost glad the stage parts hadn't been given to me; they'd have interrupted my outside work.

After a month without a thing turning up at the banks, though, I went back to my two rooms in the theatrical hotel one night, tired and discouraged, and I found Lou there. I expected him to give me another talk on dropping the whole thing; he'd been doing that for a couple of weeks now, every time we got together. I felt too low to put up an argument. But Lou was holding back his excitement—acting like a cop, you know, instead of projecting his feelings—and he couldn't haul me out to his car as fast as he probably wanted me to go.

"Been trying to get in touch with you all day, Mark. Some old guy was found wandering around, dazed and suffering from malnutrition, with $17,000 in cash inside the lining of his jacket."

"*Alive?*" I asked, shocked right into eagerness again.

"Just barely. They're trying intravenous feeding to pull him through. I don't think he'll make it."

"For God's sake, let's get there before he conks out!"

Lou raced me to the City Hospital and up to the ward. There was a scrawny old man in a bed, nothing but a papery skin stretched thin over a face like a skull and a body like a Halloween skeleton, shivering as if he was cold. I knew it wasn't the cold. The medics were injecting a heart stimulant into him and he was vibrating like a rattletrap car racing over a gravel road.

"Who are you?" I practically yelled, grabbing his skinny arm. "What happened to you?"

He went on shaking with his eyes closed and his mouth open.

"Ah, hell!" I said, disgusted. "He's in a coma."

"He might start talking," Lou told me. "I fixed it up so you can sit here and listen in case he does."

"So I can listen to delirious ravings, you mean."

Lou got me a chair and put it next to the bed. "What are you kicking about? This is the first live one you've seen, isn't it? That ought to be good enough for you." He looked as annoyed as a director. "Besides, you can get biographical data out of delirium that you'd never get if he was conscious."

*

He was right, of course. Not only data, but attitudes, wishes, resentments that would normally be repressed. I wasn't thinking of acting at the moment, though. Here was somebody who could tell me what I wanted to know ... only he couldn't talk.

Lou went to the door. "Good luck," he said, and went out.

I sat down and stared at the old man, *willing* him to talk. I don't have to ask if you've ever done that; everybody has. You keep thinking over and over, getting more and more tense, "Talk, damn you, *talk*!" until you find that every muscle in your body is a fist and your jaws are aching because you've been clenching your teeth so hard. You might just as well not bother, but once in a while a coincidence makes you think you've done it. Like now.

The old man sort of came to. That is, he opened his eyes and looked around without seeing anything, or it was so far away and long ago that nobody else could see what he saw.

I hunched forward on the chair and willed harder than ever. Nothing happened. He stared at the ceiling and through and beyond me. Then he closed his eyes again and I slumped back, defeated and bitter—but that was when he began talking.

There were a couple of women, though they might have been little girls in his childhood, and he had his troubles with them. He was praying for a toy train, a roadster, to pass his tests, to keep from being fired, to be less lonely, and back to toys again. He hated his father, and his mother was too busy with church bazaars and such to pay much attention to him. There was a sister: she died when he was a kid. He was glad she died, hoping maybe now his mother would notice him, but he was also filled with guilt because he was glad. Then somebody, he felt, was trying to shove him out of his job.

The intravenous feeding kept dripping into his vein and he went on rambling. After ten or fifteen minutes of it, he fell asleep. I felt so disappointed that I could have slapped him awake, only it wouldn't have done any good. Smoking would have helped me relax, but it wasn't allowed, and I didn't dare go outside for one, for fear he might revive again and this time come up to the present.

*

Broke!" he suddenly shrieked, trying to sit up.

I pushed him down gently, and he went on in frightful terror, "Old and poor, nowhere to go, nobody wants me, can't make a living, read the ads every day, no jobs for old men."

He blurted through weeks, months, years—I don't know—of fear and despair. And finally he came to something that made his face glow like a radium dial.

"An ad. No experience needed. Good salary." His face got dark and awful. All he added was, "El Greco," or something that sounded like it, and then he went into terminal breathing.

I rang for the nurse and she went for the doctor. I couldn't stand the long moments when the old man's chest stopped moving, the abrupt frantic gulps of air followed by no breath at all. I wanted to get away from it, but I had to wait for whatever more he might say.

It didn't come. His eyes fogged and rolled up and he stopped taking those spasmodic strangling breaths. The nurse came back with the doctor, who felt his pulse and shook his head. She pulled the blanket over the old man's face.

I left, feeling sick. I'd learned things I already knew about hate and love and fear and hope and frustration. There was an ad in it somewhere, but I had no way of telling if it had been years ago or recently. And a name that sounded like "El Greco." That was a Spanish painter of four-five hundred years ago. Had the old guy been remembering a picture he'd seen?

No, he'd come up at least close to the present. The ad seemed to solve his problem about being broke. But what about the $17,000 that had been found in the lining of his jacket? He hadn't mentioned that. Of course, being a senile psychotic, he could have considered himself broke even with that amount of money. None coming in, you see.

That didn't add up, either. His was the terror of being old and jobless. If he'd had money, he would have figured how to make it last, and that would have come through in one way or another.

There was the ad, there was his hope, and there was this El Greco. A Greek restaurant, maybe, where he might have been bumming his meals.

But where did the $17,000 fit in?

*

Lou Pape was too fed up with the whole thing to discuss it with me. He just gave me the weary eye and said, "You're riding this too hard, Mark. The guy was talking from fever. How do I know what figures and what doesn't when I'm dealing with insanity or delirium?"

"But you admit there's plenty about these cases that doesn't figure?"

"Sure. Did you take a look at the condition the world is in lately? Why should these old people be any exception?"

I couldn't blame him. He'd pulled me in on the cases with plenty of trouble to himself, just to do me a favor. Now he was fed up. I guess it wasn't even that—he thought I was ruining myself, at least financially and maybe worse, by trying to run down the problem. He said he'd be glad to see me any time and gas about anything or help me with whatever might be bothering me, if he could, but not these cases any more. He told me to lay off them, and then he left me on my own.

I don't know what he could have done, actually. I didn't need him to go through the want ads with me, which I was doing every day, figuring there might be something in the ravings about an ad. I spent more time than I liked checking those slanted at old people, only to find they were supposed to become messengers and such.

One brought me to an old brownstone five-story house in the East 80s. I got on line with the rest of the applicants—there were men and women, all decrepit, all looking badly in need of money—and waited my turn. My face was lined with collodion wrinkles and I wore an antique shiny suit and rundown shoes. I didn't look more prosperous or any younger than they did.

I finally came up to the woman who was doing the interviewing. She sat behind a plain office desk down in the main floor hall, with a pile of application cards in front of her and a ballpoint pen in one strong, slender hand. She had red hair with gold lights in it and eyes so pale blue that they would have seemed the same color as the whites if she'd been on the stage. Her face would have been beautiful except for her rigid control of expression; she smiled abruptly, shut it off just like that, looked me over with all the impersonality and penetration of an X-ray from the soles to the bald head, exactly as she'd done with the others. But that skin! If it was as perfect as that all over her slim, stiffly erect, proudly shaped body, she had no business off the stage!

"Name, address, previous occupation, social security number?" she asked in a voice with good clarity, resonance and diction. She wrote it all down while I gave the information to her. Then she asked me for references, and I mentioned Sergeant Lou Pape. "Fine," she said. "We'll get in touch with you if anything comes up. Don't call us—we'll call you."

I hung around to see who'd be picked. There was only one, an old man, two ahead of me in the line, who had no social security number, no references, not even any relatives or friends she could have checked up on him with.

Damn! *Of course* that was what she wanted! Hadn't all the starvation cases been people without social security, references, either no friends and relatives or those they'd lost track of?

I'd pulled a blooper, but how was I to know until too late?

Well, there was a way of making it right.

*

When it was good and dark that evening, I stood on the corner and watched the lights in the brownstone house. The ones on the first two floors went out, leaving only those on the third and fourth. Closed for the day ... or open for business?

I got into a building a few doors down by pushing a button and waiting until the buzzer answered, then racing up to the roof while some man yelled down the stairs to find out who was there. I crossed the tops of the two houses between and went down the fire escape.

It wasn't easy, though not as tough as you might imagine. The fact is that I'm a whole year younger than Lou Pape, even if I could play his grandpa professionally. I still have muscles left and I used them to get down the fire escape at the rear of the house.

The fourth floor room I looked into had some kind of wire mesh cage and some hooded machinery. Nobody there.

The third floor room was the redhead's. She was coming out of the bathroom with a terrycloth bathrobe and a towel turban on when I looked in. She slid the robe off and began dusting herself with powder. That skin *did* cover her.

She turned and moved toward a vanity against the wall that I was on the other side of. The next thing I knew, the window was flung up and she had a gun on me.

"Come right in—Mr. Weldon, isn't it?" she said in that completely controlled voice of hers. One day her control would crack, I thought irrelevantly, and the pieces would be found from Dallas to North Carolina. "I had an idea you seemed more curious than was justified by a help-wanted ad."

"A man my age doesn't get to see many pretty girls," I told her, making my own voice crack pathetically in a senile whinny.

She motioned me into the room. When I was inside, I saw a light over the window blinking red. It stopped the moment I was in the room. A silent burglar alarm.

She let her pale blue eyes wash insolently over me. "A man your age can see all the pretty girls he wants to. You're not old."

"And you use a rinse," I retorted.

She ignored it. "I specifically advertised for old people. Why did you apply?"

It had happened so abruptly that I hadn't had a chance to use the Stanislavsky method to *feel* old in the presence of a beautiful nude woman. I don't even know if it would have worked. Nothing's perfect.

"I needed a job awful bad," I answered sullenly, knowing it sounded like an ad lib.

*

She smiled with more contempt than humor. "You had a job, Mr. Weldon. You were very busy trying to find out why senile psychotics starve themselves to death."

"How did you know that?" I asked, startled.

"A little investigation of my own. I also happen to know you didn't tell your friend Sergeant Pape that you were going to be here tonight."

That was a fact, too. I hadn't felt sure enough that I'd found the answer to call him about it. Looking at the gun in her steady hand, I was sorry I hadn't.

"But you did find out I own this building, that my name is May Roberts, and that I'm the daughter of the late Dr. Anthony Roberts, the physicist," she continued. "Is there anything else you want me to tell you about yourself?"

"I know enough already. I'm more interested in you and the starvation cases. If you weren't connected with them, you wouldn't have known I was investigating them."

"That's obvious, isn't it?" She reached for a cigarette on the vanity and used a lighter with her free hand. The big mirror gave me another view of her lovely body, but that was beginning to interest me less than the gun. I thought of making a grab for it. There was too much distance between us, though, and she knew better than to take her eyes off me while she was lighting up. "I'm not afraid of professional detectives, Mr. Weldon. They deal only with facts and every one of them will draw the same conclusions from a given set of circumstances. I don't like amateurs. They guess too much. They don't stick to reality. The result—" her pale eyes chilled and her shapely mouth went hard—"is that they are likely to get too close to the truth."

I wanted a smoke myself, but I wasn't willing to make a move toward the pipe in my jacket. "I may be close to the truth, Miss Roberts, but I don't know what the devil it is. I still don't know how you're tied in with the senile psychotics or why they starve with all that money. You could let me go and I wouldn't have a thing on you."

She glanced down at herself and laughed for real for the first time. "You wouldn't, would you? On the other hand, you know where I'm working from and could nag Sergeant Pape into getting a search warrant. It wouldn't incriminate me, but it would be inconvenient. I don't care to be inconvenienced."

"Which means what?"

"You want to find out my connection with senile psychotics. I intend to show you."

"How?"

She gestured dangerously with the gun. "Turn your face to the wall and stay that way while I get dressed. Make one attempt to turn around before I tell you to and I'll shoot you. You're guilty of housebreaking, you know. It would be a little inconvenient for me to have an investigation ... but not as inconvenient as for you."

*

I faced the wall, feeling my stomach braid itself into a tight, painful knot of fear. Of what, I didn't know yet, only that old people who had something to do with her died of starvation. I wasn't old, but that didn't seem very comforting. She was the most frigid, calculating, *deadly* woman I'd ever met. That alone was enough to scare hell out of me. And there was the problem of what she was capable of.

Hearing the sounds of her dressing behind me, I wanted to lunge around and rush her, taking a chance that she might be too busy pulling on a girdle or reaching back to fasten a bra to have the gun in her hand. It was a suicidal impulse and I gave it up instantly. Other women might compulsively finish concealing themselves before snatching up the gun. Not her.

"All right," she said at last.

I faced her. She was wearing coveralls that, if anything, emphasized the curves of her figure. She had a sort of babushka that covered her red hair and kept it in place—the kind of thing women workers used to wear in factories during the war. She had looked lethal with nothing on but a gun and a hard expression. She looked like a sentence of execution now.

"Open that door, turn to the right and go upstairs," she told me, indicating directions with the gun.

I went. It was the longest, most anxious short walk I've ever taken. She ordered me to open a door on the fourth floor, and we were inside the room I'd seen from the fire escape. The mesh cage seemed like a torture chamber to me, the hooded motors designed to shoot an agonizing current through my emaciating body.

"You're going to do to me what you did to the old man you hired today?" I probed, hoping for an answer that would really answer.

She flipped on the switch that started the motors and there was a shrill, menacing whine. The wire mesh of the cage began blurring oddly, as if vibrating like the tines of a tuning fork.

"You've been an unexpected nuisance, Weldon," she said above the motors. "I never thought you'd get this far. But as long as you have, we might as well both benefit by it."

"Benefit?" I repeated. "*Both* of us?"

She opened the drawer of a work table and pulled out a stack of envelopes held with a rubber band. She put the stack at the other edge of the table.

"Would you rather have all cash or bank accounts or both?"

My heart began to beat. *She was where the money came from!*

*

You trying to tell me you're a philanthropist?" I demanded.

"Business is philanthropy, in a way," she answered calmly. "You need money and I need your services. To that extent, we're doing each other a favor. I think you'll find that the favor I'm going to do for you is a pretty considerable one. Would you mind picking up the envelopes on the table?"

I took the stack and stared at the top envelope. "May 15, 1931," I read aloud, and looked suspiciously at her. "What's this for?"

"I don't think it's something that can be explained. At least it's never been possible before and I doubt if it would be now. I'm assuming you want both cash and bank accounts. Is that right?"

"Well, yes. Only—"

"We'll discuss it later." She looked along a row of shelves against one wall, searching the labels on the stacks of bundles there. She drew one out and pushed it toward me. "Please open that and put on the things you'll find inside."

I tore open the bundle. It contained a very plain business suit, black shoes, shirt, tie and a hat with a narrow brim.

"Are these supposed to be my burial clothes?"

"I asked you to put them on," she said. "If you want me to make that a command, I'll do it."

I looked at the gun and I looked at the clothes and then for some shelter I could change behind. There wasn't any.

She smiled. "You didn't seem concerned about my modesty. I don't see why your own should bother you. Get dressed!"

I obeyed, my mind anxiously chasing one possibility after another, all of them ending up with my death. I got into the other things and felt even more uncomfortable. They were all only an approximate fit: the shoes a little too tight and pointed, the collar of the shirt too stiffly starched and too high under my chin, the gray suit too narrow at the shoulders and the ankles. I wished I had a mirror to see myself in. I felt like an ultra-conservative Wall Street broker and I was sure I resembled one.

"All right," she said. "Put the envelopes in your inside pocket. You'll find instructions on each. Follow them carefully."

"I don't get it!" I protested.

"You will. Now step into the mesh cage. Use the envelopes in the order they're arranged in."

"But what's this all about?"

"I can tell you just one thing, Mr. Weldon—don't try to escape. It can't be done. Your other questions will answer themselves if you follow the instructions on the envelopes."

She had the gun in her hand. I went into the mesh cage, not knowing what to expect and yet too afraid of her to refuse. I didn't want to wind up dead of starvation, no matter how much money she might have given me—but I didn't want to get shot, either.

She closed the mesh gate and pushed the switch as far as it would go. The motors screamed as they picked up speed; the mesh cage vibrated more swiftly; I could see her through it as if there were nothing between us.

And then I couldn't see her at all.

I was outside a bank on a sunny day in spring.

*

My fear evaporated instantly—I'd escaped somehow!

But then a couple of realizations slapped me from each side. It was day instead of night. I was out on the street and not in her brownstone house.

Even the season had changed!

Dazed, I stared at the people passing by. They looked like characters in a TV movie, the women wearing long dresses and flowerpot hats, their faces made up with petulant rosebud mouths and bright blotches of rouge; the men in hard straw hats, suits with narrow shoulders, plain black or brown shoes—the same kind of clothes I was wearing.

The rumble of traffic in the street caught me next. Cars with square bodies, tubular radiators....

For a moment, I let terror soak through me. Then I remembered the mesh cage and the motors. May Roberts could have given me electro-shock, kept me under long enough for the season to change, or taken me South and left me on a street in daylight.

But this was a street in New York. I recognized it, though some of the buildings seemed changed, the people dressed more shabbily.

Shrewd stagesetting? Hypnosis?

That was it, of course! She'd hypnotized me....

Except that a subject under hypnosis doesn't know he's been hypnotized.

Completely confused, I took out the stack of envelopes I'd put in my pocket. I was supposed to have both cash and a bank account, and I was outside a bank. She obviously wanted me to go in, so I did. I handed the top envelope to the teller.

He hauled $150 out of it and looked at me as if that was enough to buy and sell the bank. He asked me if I had an account there. I didn't. He took me over to an officer of the bank, a fellow with a Hoover collar and a John Gilbert mustache, who signed me up more cordially than I'd been treated in years.

I walked out to the street, gaping at the entry in the bankbook he'd handed me. My pulse was jumping lumpily, my lungs refusing to work right, my head doing a Hopi rain dance.

The date he'd stamped was May 15, 1931.

*

I didn't know which I was more afraid of—being stranded, middle-aged, in the worst of the depression, or being yanked back to that brownstone house. I had only an instant to realize that I was a kid in high school uptown right at that moment. Then the whole scene vanished as fast as blinking and I was outside another bank somewhere else in the city.

The date on the envelope was May 29th and it was still 1931. I made a $75 deposit there, then $100 in another place a few days later, and so forth, spending only a few minutes each time and going forward anywhere from a couple of days to almost a month.

Every now and then, I had a stamped, addressed envelope to mail at a corner box. They were addressed to different stock brokers and when I got one open before mailing it and took a look inside, it turned out to be an order to buy a few hundred shares of stock in a soft drink company in the name of Dr. Anthony Roberts. I hadn't remembered the price of the shares being that low. The last time I'd seen the quotation, it was more than five times as much as it was then. I was making dough myself, but I was doing even better for May Roberts.

A few times I had to stay around for an hour or so. There was the night I found myself in a flashy speakeasy with two envelopes that I was to bet the contents of, according to the instructions on the outside. It was June 21, 1932, and I had to bet on Jack Sharkey to take the heavyweight title away from Max Schmeling.

The place was serious and quiet—no more than three women, a couple of bartenders, and the rest male customers, including two cops, huddling up close to the radio. An affable character was taking bets. He gave me a wise little smile when I put the money down on Sharkey.

"Well, it's a pleasure to do business with a man who wants an American to win," he said, "and the hell with the smart dough, eh?"

"Yeah," I said, and tried to smile back, but so much of the smart money was going on Schmeling that I wondered if May Roberts hadn't made a mistake. I couldn't remember who had won. "You know what J. P. Morgan said—don't sell America short."

"I'll take a buck for my share," said a sour guy who barely managed to stand. "Lousy grass growing in the lousy streets, nobody working, no future, nothing!"

"We'll come out of it okay," I told him confidently.

He snorted into his gin. "Not in our lifetime, Mac. It'd take a miracle to put this country on its feet again. I don't believe in miracles." He put his scowling face up close to mine and breathed blearily and belligerently at me. "Do you?"

"Shut up, Gus," one of the bartenders said. "The fight's starting."

*

I had some tough moments and a lot of bad Scotch, listening. It went the whole 15 rounds, Sharkey won, and I was in almost as bad shape as Gus, who'd passed out halfway through the battle. All I can recall is the affable character handing over a big roll and saying, "Lucky for me more guys don't sell America short," and trying to separate the money into the right amounts and put them into the right envelopes, while stumbling out the door, when everything changed and I was outside a bank again.

I thought, "My God, what a hangover cure!" I was as sober as if I hadn't had a drink, when I made that deposit.

There were more envelopes to mail and more deposits to make and bets to put down on Singing Wood in 1933 at Belmont Park and Max Baer over Primo Carnera, and then Cavalcade at Churchill Downs in 1934, and James Braddock over Baer in 1935, and a big daily double payoff, Wanoah-Arakay at Tropical Park, and so on, skipping through the years like a flat stone over water, touching here and there for a few minutes to an hour at a time. I kept the envelopes for May Roberts and myself in different pockets and the bankbooks in another. The envelopes were beginning to bulge and the deposits and accrued interest were something to watch grow.

The whole thing, in fact, was so exciting that it was early October of 1938—a total of maybe four or five hours subjectively—before I realized what she had me doing. I wasn't thinking much about the fact that I was time traveling or how she did it; I accepted that, though the sensation in some ways was creepy, like raising the dead. My father and mother, for instance, were still alive in 1938. If I could break away from whatever it was that kept pulling me jumpily through time, I could go and see them.

The thought attracted me enough to make me shake badly with intent, yet pump dread through me. I wanted so damned badly to see them again and I didn't dare. I couldn't....

Why couldn't I?

Maybe the machine covered only the area around the various banks, speakeasies, bars and horse parlors. If I could get out of the area, whatever it might be, I could avoid coming back to whatever May Roberts had lined up for me.

Because, naturally, I knew now what I was doing: I was making deposits and winning sure bets just as the "senile psychotics" had done. The ink on their bankbooks and bills was fresh because it *was* fresh; it wasn't given a chance to oxidize—at the rate I was going, I'd be back to my own time in another few hours or so, with $15,000 or better in deposits, compound interest and cash.

If I'd been around 70, you see, she could have sent me back to the beginning of the century with the same amount of money, which would have accumulated to something like $30,000.

Get it now?

I did.

And I felt sick and frightened.

The old people had died of starvation somehow with all that dough in cash or banks. I didn't give a hang if the time travel was responsible, or something else was. I wasn't going to be found dead in my hotel and have Lou Pape curse my corpse because I'd been borrowing from him when, since 1931, I'd had a little fortune put away. He'd call me a premature senile psychotic and he'd be right, from his point of view, not knowing the truth.

*

Rather than make the deposit in October, 1938, I grabbed a battered old cab and told the driver to step on it. When I showed him the $10 bill that was in it for him, he squashed down the gas pedal. In 1938, $10 was real money.

We got a mile away from the bank and the driver looked at me in the rear-view mirror.

"How far you want to go, mister?"

My teeth were together so hard that I had to unclench them before I could answer, "As far away as we can get."

"Cops after you?"

"No, but somebody is. Don't be surprised at anything that happens, no matter what it is."

"You mean like getting shot at?" he asked worriedly, slowing down.

"You're not in any danger, friend. I am. Relax and step on it again."

I wondered if she could still reach me, this far from the bank, and handed the guy the bill. No justice sticking him for the ride in case she should. He pushed the pedal down even harder than he had been doing before.

We must have been close to three miles away when I blinked and was standing outside the first bank I'd seen in 1931.

I don't know what the cab driver thought when I vanished out of his hack. He probably figured I'd opened the door and jumped while he wasn't looking. Maybe he even went back and searched for a body splashed all over the street.

Well, it would have been a hopeless hunt. I was a week ahead.

I gave up and drearily made my deposit. The one from early October that I'd missed I put in with this one.

There was no way to escape the babe with the beautiful hard face, gorgeous warm body and plans for me that all seemed to add up to death. I didn't try any more. I went on making deposits, mailing orders to her stock brokers, and putting down bets that couldn't miss because they were all past history.

I don't even remember what the last one was, a fight or a race. I hung around the bar that had long ago replaced the speakeasy, until the inevitable payoff, got myself a hamburger and headed out the door. All the envelopes I was supposed to use were gone and I felt shaky, knowing that the next place I'd see was the room with the wire mesh cage and the hooded motors.

It was.

*

She was on the other side of the cage, and I had five bankbooks and envelopes filled with cash amounting to more than $15,000, but all I could think of was that I was hungry and something had happened to the hamburger while I was traveling through time. I must have fallen and dropped it, because my hand was covered with dust or dirt. I brushed it off and quickly felt my face and pulled up my sleeves to look at my arms.

"Very smart," I said, "but I'm nowhere near emaciation."

"What made you think you would be?" she asked.

"Because the others always were."

She cut the motors to idling speed and the vibrating mesh slowed down. I glared at her through it. God, she was lovely—as lovely as an ice sculpture! The kind of face you'd love to kiss and slap, kiss and slap....

"You came here with a preconceived notion, Mr. Weldon. I'm a businesswoman, not a monster. I like to think there's even a good deal of the altruist in me. I could hire only young people, but the old ones have more trouble finding work. And you've seen for yourself how I provide nest eggs for them they'd otherwise never have."

"And take care of yourself at the same time."

"That's the businesswoman in me. I need money to operate."

"So do the old people. Only they die and you don't."

She opened the gate and invited me out. "I make mistakes

occasionally. I sometimes pick men and women who prove to be too old to stand the strain. I try not to let it happen, but they need money and work so badly that they don't always tell the truth about their age and state of health."

"You could take those who have social security cards and references."

"But those who don't have any are in worse need!" She paused. "You probably think I want only the money you and they bring back, that it's merely some sort of profit-making scheme. It isn't."

"You mean the idea is not just to build up a fortune for you with a cut for whoever helps you do it?"

"I said I need money to operate, Mr. Weldon, and this method serves. But there are other purposes, much more important. What you have gone through is—basic training, you might say. You know now that it's possible to travel through time, and what it's like. The initial shock, in other words, is gone and you're better equipped to do something for me in another era."

"Something else?" I stared at her puzzledly. "What else could you want?"

"Let's have dinner first. You must be hungry."

*

I was, and that reminded me: "I bought a hamburger just before you brought me back. I don't know what happened to it. My hand was dirty and the hamburger was gone, as if I'd fallen somehow and dropped it and got dirt on my hand."

She looked worriedly at the hand, probably afraid I'd cut it and disqualified myself. I could understand that; you never know what kind of diseases can be picked up in different times, because I remember reading somewhere that germs keep changing according to conditions. Right now, for instance, strains of bacteria are becoming resistant to antibiotics. I knew her concern wasn't really for me, but it was pleasant all the same.

"That could be the explanation, I suppose," she said. "The truth is

that I've never taken a time voyage—somebody has to operate the
controls in the present—so I can't say it's possible or impossible to
fall. It must be, since you did. Perhaps the wrench back from the past
was too violent and you slipped just before you returned."

She led me down to an ornate dining room, where the table had
been set for two. The food was waiting on the table, steaming and
smelling tasty. Nobody was around to serve us. She pointed out a
chair to me and we sat down and began eating. I was a little nervous
at first, afraid there might be something in the food, but it tasted fine
and nothing happened after I swallowed a little and waited for some
effect.

"You did try to escape the time tractor beam, didn't you, Mr.
Weldon?" she asked. I didn't have to answer; she knew. "That's a
mistaken notion of how it functions. The control beam doesn't cover
area; it covers *era*. You could have flown to any part of the world and
the beam would still have brought you back. Do I make myself clear?"

She did. Too bloody clear. I waited for the rest.

"I assume you've already formed an opinion of me," she went on.
"A rather unflattering one, I imagine."

"'Bitch' is the cleanest word I can find. But a clever one. Anybody
who can invent a time machine would have to be a genius."

"I didn't invent it. My father did—Dr. Anthony Roberts—using the
funds you and others helped me provide him with." Her face grew
soft and tender. "My father was a wonderful man, a great man, but he
was called a crackpot. He was kept from teaching or working
anywhere. It was just as well, I suppose, though he was too hurt to
think so; he had more leisure to develop the time machine. He could
have used it to extort repayment from mankind for his humiliation,
but he didn't. He used it to help mankind."

"Like how?" I goaded.

"It doesn't matter, Mr. Weldon. You're determined to hate me and
consider me a liar. Nothing I tell you can change that."

*

30

She was right about the first part—I hadn't dared let myself do anything except hate and fear her—but she was wrong about the second. I remembered thinking how Lou Pape would have felt if I had died of starvation with over $15,000, after borrowing from him all the time between jobs. Not knowing how I got it, he'd have been sore, thinking I'd played him for a patsy. What I'm trying to say is that Lou wouldn't have had enough information to judge me. I didn't have enough information yet, either, to judge her.

"What do you want me to do?" I asked warily.

"Everybody but one person was sent into the past on specific errands—to save art treasures and relics that would otherwise have been lost to humanity."

"Not because the things might be worth a lot of dough?" I said nastily.

"You've already seen that I can get all the money I want. There were upheavals in the past—great fires, wars, revolutions, vandalism—and I had my associates save things that would have been destroyed. Oh, beautiful things, Mr. Weldon! The world would have been so much poorer without them!"

"El Greco, for instance?" I asked, remembering the raving old man who had been found wandering with $17,000 in his coat lining.

"El Greco, too. Several paintings that had been lost for centuries." She became more brisk and efficient-seeming. "Except for the one man I mentioned, I concentrated on the past—the future is too completely unknown to us. And there's an additional reason why I tentatively explored it only once. But the one person who went there discovered something that would be of immense value to the world."

"What happened to *him*?"

She looked regretful. "He was too old. He survived just long enough to tell me that the future has something we need. It's a metal box, small enough to carry, that could supply this whole city with power to run its industries and light its homes and streets!"

"Sounds good. Who'd you say benefits if I get it?"

"We share the profits equally, of course. But it must be understood that we sell the power so cheaply that everybody can afford it."

"I'm not arguing. What's the other reason you didn't bother with the future?"

"You can't bring anything from the future to the present that doesn't exist right now. I won't go into the theory, but it should be obvious that nothing can exist before it exists. You can't bring the box I want, only the technical data to build one."

"Technical data? I'm an actor, not a scientist."

"You'll have pens and weatherproof notebooks to copy it down in."

*

I couldn't make up my mind about her. I've already said she was beautiful, which always prejudices a man in a woman's favor, but I couldn't forget the starvation cases. They hadn't shared anything but malnutrition, useless money and death. Then again, maybe her explanation was a good one, that she wanted to help those who needed help most and some of them lied about their age and physical condition because they wanted the jobs so badly. All I knew about were those who had died. How did I know there weren't others—a lot more of them than the fatal cases, perhaps—who came through all right and were able to enjoy their little fortunes?

And there was her story about saving the treasures of the past and wanting to provide power at really low cost. She was right about one thing: she didn't need any of that to make money with; her method was plenty good enough, using the actual records of the past to invest in stocks, bet on sports—all sure gambles.

But those starvation cases....

"Do I get any guarantees?" I demanded.

She looked annoyed. "I'll need you for the data. You'll need me to turn it into manufacture. Is that enough of a guarantee?"

"No. Do I come out of this alive?"

"Mr. Weldon, please use some logic. I'm the one who's taking the risk. I've already given you more money than you've ever had at one time in your life. Part of my motive was to pay for services about to be rendered. Mostly, it was to give you experience in traveling through time."

"And to prove to me that I can't run out," I added.

"That happens to be a necessary attribute of the machine. I couldn't very well move you about through time unless it worked that way. If you'd look at my point of view, you'd see that I lose my investment if you don't bring back the data. I can't withdraw your money, you realize."

"I don't know what to think," I said, dissatisfied with myself because I couldn't find out what, if anything, was wrong with the deal. "I'll get you the data for the power box if it's at all possible and then we'll see what happens."

Finished eating, we went upstairs and I got into the cage.

She closed the circuit. The motors screamed. The mesh blurred.

And I was in a world I never knew.

*

You'd call it a city, I suppose; there were enough buildings to make it one. But no city ever had so much greenery. It wasn't just tree-lined streets, like Unter den Linden in Berlin, or islands covered with shrubbery, like Park Avenue in New York. The grass and trees and shrubs grew around every building, separating them from each other by wide lawns. The buildings were more glass—or what looked like glass—than anything else. A few of the windows were opaque against the sun, but I couldn't see any shades or blinds. Some kind of polarizing glass or plastic?

I felt uneasy being there, but it was a thrill just the same, to be alive in the future when I and everybody who lived in my day was supposed to be dead.

The air smelled like the country. There was no foul gas boiling from the teardrop cars on the glass-level road. They were made of transparent plastic clear around and from top to bottom, and they moved along at a fair clip, but more smoothly than swiftly. If I hadn't seen the airship overhead, I wouldn't have known it was there. It flew silently, a graceful ball without wings, seeming to be borne by the wind from one horizon to the other, except that no wind ever moved that fast.

One car stopped nearby and someone shouted, "Here we are!" Several people leaped out and headed for me.

I didn't think. I ran. I crossed the lawn and ducked into the nearest building and dodged through long, smoothly walled, shadowlessly lit corridors until I found a door that would open. I slammed it shut and locked it. Then, panting, I fell into a soft chair that seemed to form itself around my body, and felt like kicking myself for the bloody idiot I was.

What in hell had I run for? They couldn't have known who I was. If I'd arrived in a time when people wore togas or bathing suits, there would have been some reason for singling me out, but they had all had clothes just like ours—suits and shirts and ties for the men, a dress and high heels for the one woman with them. I felt somewhat disappointed that clothes hadn't changed any, but it worked out to my advantage; I wouldn't be so conspicuous.

Yet why should anyone have yelled "Here we are!" unless.... No, they must have thought I was somebody else. It didn't figure any other way. I had run because it was my first startled reaction and probably because I knew I was there on what might be considered illegal business; if I succeeded, some poor inventor would be done out of his royalties.

I wished I hadn't run. Besides making me feel like a scared fool, I was sweaty and out of breath. Playing old men doesn't make climbing down fire escapes much tougher than it should be, but it doesn't exactly make a sprinter out of you—not by several lungfuls.

*

I sat there, breathing hard and trying to guess what next. I had no more idea of where to go for what I wanted than an ancient Egyptian set down in the middle of Times Square with instructions to sneak a mummy out of the Metropolitan Museum. I didn't even have that much information. I didn't know any part of the city, how it was laid out, or where to get the data that May Roberts had sent me for.

I opened the door quietly and looked both ways before going out. After losing myself in the cross-connecting corridors a few times, I finally came to an outside door. I stopped, tense, trying to get my courage. My inclination was to slip, sneak or dart out, but I made myself walk away like a decent, innocent citizen. That was one disguise they'd never be able to crack. All I had to do was act as if I belonged to that time and place and who would know the difference?

There were other people walking as if they were in no hurry to get anywhere. I slowed down to their speed, but I wished wistfully that there was a crowd to dive into and get lost.

A man dropped into step and said politely, "I beg your pardon. Are you a stranger in town?"

I almost halted in alarm, but that might have been a giveaway. "What makes you think so?" I asked, forcing myself to keep at the same easy pace.

"I—didn't recognize your face and I thought—"

"It's a big city," I said coldly. "You can't know everyone."

"If there's anything I can do to help—"

I told him there wasn't and left him standing there. It was plain common sense, I had decided quickly while he was talking to me, not to take any risks by admitting anything. I might have been dumped into a police state or the country could have been at war without my knowing it, or maybe they were suspicious of strangers. For one reason or another, ranging from vagrancy to espionage, I could be pulled in, tortured, executed, God knows what. The place looked peaceful enough, but that didn't prove a thing.

I went on walking, looking for something I couldn't be sure existed, in a city I was completely unfamiliar with, in a time when I had no right to be alive. It wasn't just a matter of getting the information she wanted. I'd have been satisfied to hang around until she pulled me back without the data....

But then what would happen? Maybe the starvation cases were people who had failed her! For that matter, she could shoot me and send the remains anywhere in time to get rid of the evidence.

Damn it, I didn't know if she was better or worse than I'd supposed, but I wasn't going to take any chances. I had to bring her what she wanted.

*

There was a sign up ahead. It read: TO SHOPPING CENTER. The arrow pointed along the road. When I came to a fork and wondered which way to go, there was another sign, then another pointing to still more farther on.

I followed them to the middle of the city, a big square with a park in the center and shops of all kinds rimming it. The only shop I was interested in said: ELECTRICAL APPLIANCES.

I went in.

A neat young salesman came up and politely asked me if he could do anything for me. I sounded stupid even to myself, but I said, "No, thanks, I'd just like to do a little browsing," and gave a silly nervous laugh. Me, an actor, behaving like a frightened yokel! I felt ashamed of myself.

He tried not to look surprised, but he didn't really succeed. Somebody else came in, though, for which I was grateful, and he left me alone to look around.

I don't know if I can get my feelings across to you. It's a situation that nobody would ever expect to find himself in, so it isn't easy to tell what it's like. But I've got to try.

Let's stick with the ancient Egyptian I mentioned a while back, the one ordered to sneak a mummy out of the Metropolitan Museum. Maybe that'll make it clearer.

The poor guy has no money he can use, naturally, and no idea of what New York's transportation system is like, where the museum is, how to get there, what visitors to a museum do and say, the regulations he might unwittingly break, how much an ordinary citizen is supposed to know about which customs and such. Now add the possible danger that he might be slapped into jail or an insane asylum if he makes a mistake and you've got a rough notion of the spot I felt I was in. Being able to speak English doesn't make much difference; not knowing what's regarded as right and wrong, and the unknown consequences, are enough to panic anybody.

That doesn't make it clear enough.

Well, look, take the electrical appliances in that store; that might give you an idea of the situation and the way it affected me.

The appliances must have been as familiar to the people of that time as toasters and TV sets and lamps are to us. But the things didn't make a bit of sense to me ... any more than our appliances would to the ancient Egyptian. Can you imagine him trying to figure out what those items are for and how they work?

*

Here are some gadgets you can puzzle over:

There was a light fixture that you put against any part of a wall—no screws, no cement, no wires, even—and it held there and lit up, and it stayed lit no matter where you moved it on the wall. Talk about pin-up lamps ... this was really it!

Then I came across something that looked like an ashtray with a blue electric shimmer obscuring the bottom of the bowl. I lit my pipe—others I'd passed had been smoking, so I knew it was safe to do the same—and flicked in the match. It disappeared. I don't mean it was swirled into some hidden compartment. It *vanished.* I emptied the pipe into the ashtray and that went, too. Looking around to make sure nobody was watching, I dredged some coins out of my pocket and let them drop into the tray. They were gone. Not a particle of them was left. A disintegrator? I haven't got the slightest idea.

There were little mirror boxes with three tiny dials on the front of each. I turned the dials on one—it was like using three dial telephones at the same time—and a pretty girl's face popped onto the mirror surface and looked expectantly at me.

"Yes?" she said, and waited for me to answer.

"I—uh—wrong number, I guess," I answered, putting the box down in a hurry and going to the other side of the shop because I didn't have even a dim notion how to turn it off.

The thing I was looking for was on a counter—a tinted metal box no bigger than a suitcase, with a lipped hole on top and small undisguised verniers in front. I didn't know I'd found it, actually, until I twisted a vernier and every light in the store suddenly glared and the salesman came rushing over and politely moved me aside to shut it off.

"We don't want to burn out every appliance in the place, do we?" he asked quietly.

"I just wanted to see if it worked all right," I said, still shaking slightly. It could have blown up or electrocuted me, for all I knew.

"But they always work," he said.

"Ah—always?"

"Of course. The principle is simple and there are no parts to get worn out, so they last indefinitely." He suddenly smiled as if he'd just caught the gist. "Oh, you were joking! Naturally—everybody learns about the Dynapack in primary education. You were interested in acquiring one?"

"No, no. The—the old one is good enough. I was just—well, you know, interested in knowing if the new models are much different or better than the old ones."

"But there haven't been any new models since 2073," he said. "Can you think of any reason why there should be?"

"I—guess not," I stammered. "But you never can tell."

"You can with Dynapacks," he said, and he would have gone on if I hadn't lost my nerve and mumbled my way out of the store as fast as I could.

*

You want to know why? He'd asked me if I wanted to "acquire" a Dynapack, not *buy* one. I didn't know what "acquire" meant in that society. It could be anything from saving up coupons to winning whatever you wanted at some kind of lottery, or maybe working up the right number of labor units on the job—in which case he'd want to know where I was employed and the equivalent of social security and similar information, which I naturally didn't have—or it could just be fancy sales talk for buying.

I couldn't guess, and I didn't care to expose myself any more than I had already. And my blunder about the Dynapack working and the new models was nothing to make me feel at all easier.

Lord, the uncertainties and hazards of being in a world you don't know anything about! Daydreaming about visiting another age may be pleasant, but the reality is something else again.

"Wait a minute, friend!" I heard the salesman call out behind me.

*

I looked back as casually, I hoped, as the pedestrians who heard him. He was walking quickly toward me with a very worried expression on his face. I stepped up my own pace as unobtrusively as possible, trying to keep a lot of people between us, meanwhile praying that they'd think I was just somebody who was late for an appointment. The salesman didn't break into a run or yell for the cops, but I couldn't be sure he wouldn't.

As soon as I came to a corner, I turned it and ran like hell. There was a sort of alley down the block. I jumped into it, found a basement door and stayed inside, pressed against the wall, quivering with tension and sucking air like a swimmer who'd stayed underwater too long.

Even after I got my wind back, I wasn't anxious to go out. The place could have been cordoned off, with the police, the army and the navy all cooperating to nab me.

What made me think so? Not a thing except remembering how

puzzled our ancient Egyptian would have been if he got arrested in the subway for something everybody did casually and without punishment in his own time—spitting! I could have done something just as innocent, as far as you and I are concerned, that this era would consider a misdemeanor or a major crime. And in what age was ignorance of the law ever an excuse?

Instead of going back out, I prowled carefully into the building. It was strangely silent and deserted. I couldn't understand why until I came to a lavatory. There were little commodes and wash basins that came up to barely above my knees. The place was a school. Naturally it was deserted—the kids were through for the day.

I could feel the tension dissolve in me like a ramrod of ice melting, no longer keeping my back and neck stiff and taut. There probably wasn't a better place in the city for me to hide.

A *primary school!*

The salesman had said to me, "Everybody learns about the Dynapack in primary education."

*

Going through the school was eerie, like visiting a familiar childhood scene that had been distorted by time into something almost totally unrecognizable.

There were no blackboards, teacher's big desk, children's little desks, inkwells, pointers, globes or books. Yet it was a school. The small fixtures in the lavatory downstairs had told me that, and so did the miniature chairs drawn neatly under the low, vividly painted tables in the various schoolrooms. A large comfortable chair was evidently where the teacher sat when not wandering around among the pupils.

In front of each chair, firmly attached to the table, was a box with a screen, and both sides of the box held spools of wire on blunt little spindles. The spools had large, clear numbers on them. Near the teacher's chair was a compact case with more spools on spindles, and there was a large screen on the inside wall, opposite the enormous windows.

I went into one of the rooms and sat down in the teacher's chair, wondering how I was going to find out about the Dynapack. I felt like an archaeologist guessing at the functions of strange relics he'd found in a dead city.

Sitting in the chair was like sitting on a column of air that let me sit upright or slump as I chose. One of the arms had a row of buttons. I pressed one and waited nervously to find out if I'd done something that would get me into trouble.

Concealed lights in the ceiling and walls began glowing, getting brighter, while the room gradually turned dark. I glanced around bewilderedly to see why, because it was still daylight.

The windows seemed to be sliding slightly, very slowly, and as they slid, the sunlight was damped out. I grinned, thinking of what my ancient Egyptian would make of that. I knew there were two sheets of polarizing glass, probably with a vacuum between to keep out the cold and the heat, and the lights in the room were beautifully synchronized with the polarized sliding glass.

I wasn't doing so badly. The rest of the objects might not be too hard to figure out.

The spools in the case alongside the teacher's chair could be wire recordings. I looked for something to play them with, but there was no sign of a playback machine. I tried to lift a spool off a spindle. It wouldn't come off.

Hah! The wire led down the spindle to the base of the box, holding the spool in place. That meant the spools could be played right in that position. But what started them playing?

*

I hunted over the box minutely. Every part of it was featureless—no dials, switches or any unfamiliar counterparts. I even tried moving my hands over it, figuring it might be like a theramin, and spoke to it in different shades of command, because it could have been built to respond to vocal orders. Nothing happened.

Remember the Poe story that shows the best place to hide something is right out in the open, which is the last place anyone would look? Well, these things weren't manufactured to baffle people, any more than our devices generally are. But it's only by trying everything that somebody who didn't know what a switch is would start up a vacuum cleaner, say, or light a big chandelier from a wall clear across the room.

I'd pressed every inch of the box, hoping some part of it might act as a switch, and I finally touched one of the spindles. The spool immediately began spinning at a very low speed and the screen on the wall opposite the window glowed into life.

"The history of the exploration of the Solar System," said an announcer's deep voice, "is one of the most adventuresome in mankind's long list of achievements. Beginning with the crude rockets developed during World War II...."

There were newsreel shots of V-1 and V-2 being blasted from their takeoff ramps and a montage of later experimental models. I wished I could see how it all turned out, but I was afraid to waste the time watching. At any moment, I might hear the footsteps of a guard or janitor or whoever tended buildings then.

I pushed the spindle again. It checked the spool, which rewound swiftly and silently, and stopped itself when the rewinding was finished. I tried another. A nightmare underwater scene appeared.

"With the aid of energy screens," said another voice, "the oceans of the world were completely charted by the year 2027...."

I turned it off, then another on developments in medicine, one on architecture, one on history, the geography of such places as the interior of South America and Africa that were—or are—unknown today, and I was getting frantic, starting the wonderful wire films that held full-frequency sound and pictures in absolutely faithful color, and shutting them off hastily when I discovered they didn't have what I was looking for.

They were courses for children, but they all contained information that our scientists are still groping for ... and I couldn't chance watching one all the way through!

I was frustratedly switching off a film on psychology when a female voice said from the door, "May I help you?"

*

I snapped around to face her in sudden fright. She was young and slim and slight, but she could scream loud enough to get help. Judging by the way she was looking at me, outwardly polite and yet visibly nervous, that scream would be coming at any second.

"I must have wandered in here by mistake," I said, and pushed past her to the corridor, where I began running back the way I had come.

"But you don't understand!" she cried after me. "I really want to help—"

Yeah, help, I thought, pounding toward the street door. A gag right out of that psychology film, probably—get the patient to hold still, humor him, until you can get somebody to put him where he belongs. That's what one of our teachers would do, provided she wasn't too scared to think straight, if she found an old-looking guy thumbing frenziedly through the textbooks in a grammar school classroom.

When I came to the outside door, I stopped. I had no way of knowing whether she'd given out an alarm, or how she might have done it, but the obvious place to find me would be out on the street, dodging for cover somewhere.

I pushed the door open and let it slam shut, hoping she'd hear it upstairs. Then I found a door, sneaked it open and went silently down the steps.

In the basement, I looked for a furnace or a coal bin or a fuel tank to hide behind, but there weren't any. I don't know how they got their heat in the winter or cooled the building in the summer. Probably some central atomic plant that took care of the whole city, piping in the heat or coolant in underground conduits that were led up through the walls, because there weren't even any pipes visible.

I hunched into the darkest corner I could find and hoped they wouldn't look for me there.

*

By the time night came, hunger drove me out of the school, but I did it warily, making sure nobody was in sight.

The streets of the shopping center were more or less deserted. There was no sign of a restaurant. I was so empty that I felt dizzy as I hunted for one. But then a shocking realization made me halt on the sidewalk and sweat with horror.

Even if there had been a restaurant, what would I have used for money?

Now I got the whole foul picture. She had sent old people back through time on errands like mine ... and they'd starved to death because they couldn't buy food!

No, that wasn't right. I remembered what I had told Lou Pape: anybody who gets hungry enough can always find a truck garden or a food store to rob.

Only ... I hadn't seen a truck garden or food store anywhere in this city.

And ... I thought about people in the past having their hands cut off for stealing a loaf of bread.

This civilization didn't look as if it went in for such drastic punishments, assuming I could find a loaf of bread to steal. But neither did most of the civilizations that practiced those barbarisms.

I was more tired, hungry and scared than I'd ever believed a human being could get. Lost, completely lost in a totally alien world, but one in which I could still be killed or starve to death ... and God knew what was waiting for me in my own time in case I came back without the information she wanted.

Or maybe even if I came back with it!

That suspicion made up my mind for me. Whatever happened to me now couldn't be worse than what she might do. At least I didn't have to starve.

I stopped a man in the street. I let several others go by before picking him deliberately because he was middle-aged, had a kindly face, and was smaller than me, so I could slug him and run if he raised a row.

"Look, friend," I told him, "I'm just passing through town—"

"Ah?" he said pleasantly.

"—And I seem to have mislaid—" No, that was dangerous. I'd been about to say I'd mislaid my wallet, but I still didn't know whether they used money in this era. He waited with a patient, friendly smile while I decided just how to put it. "The fact is that I haven't eaten all day and I wonder if you could help me get a meal."

He said in the most neighborly voice imaginable, "I'll be glad to do anything I can, Mr. Weldon."

*

My entire face seemed to drop open. "You—you called me—"

"Mr. Weldon," he repeated, still looking up at me with that neighborly smile. "Mark Weldon, isn't it? From the 20th Century?"

I tried to answer, but my throat had tightened up worse than on any opening night I'd ever had to live through. I nodded, wondering terrifiedly what was going on.

"Please relax," he said persuasively. "You're not in any danger whatever. We offer you our utmost hospitality. Our time, you might say, is your time."

"You know who I am," I managed to get out through my constricted glottis. "I've been doing all this running and ducking and hiding for nothing."

He shrugged sympathetically. "Everyone in the city was instructed to help you, but you were so nervous that we were afraid to alarm you with a direct approach. Every time we tried to, as a matter of fact, you vanished into one place or another. We didn't follow for fear of the effect on you. We had to wait until you came voluntarily to us."

My brain was racing again and getting nowhere. Part of it was dizziness from hunger, but only part. The rest was plain frightened confusion.

They knew who I was. They'd been expecting me. They probably even knew what I was after.

And they wanted to help!

"Let's not go into explanations now," he said, "although I'd like to smooth away the bewilderment and fear on your face. But you need to be fed first. Then we'll call in the others and—"

I pulled back. "What others? How do I know you're not setting up something for me that I'll wish I hadn't gotten into?"

"Before you approached me, Mr. Weldon, you first had to decide that we represented no greater menace than May Roberts. Please believe me, we don't."

So he knew about that, too!

"All right, I'll take my chances," I gave in resignedly. "Where does a guy find a place to eat in this city?"

*

It was a handsome restaurant with soft light coming from three-dimensional, full-color nature murals that I might mistakenly have walked into if I'd been alone, they looked so much like gardens and forests and plains. It was no wonder I couldn't find a restaurant or food store or truck garden anywhere—food came up through pneumatic chutes in each building, I'd been told on the way over, grown in hydroponic tanks in cities that specialized in agriculture, and those who wanted to eat "out" could drop into the restaurant each building had. Every city had its own function. This one was for people in the arts. I liked that.

There was a glowing menu on the table with buttons alongside the various selections. I looked starvingly at the items, trying to decide which I wanted most. I picked oysters, onion soup, breast of guinea hen under Plexiglas and was hunting for the tastiest and most recognizable dessert when the pleasant little guy shook his head regretfully and emphatically.

"I'm afraid you can't eat any of those foods, Mr. Weldon," he said in a sad voice. "We'll explain why in a moment."

A waiter and the manager came over. They obviously didn't want to stare at me, but they couldn't help it. I couldn't blame them, I'd have stared at somebody from George Washington's time, which is about what I must have represented to them.

"Will you please arrange to have the special food for Mr. Weldon delivered here immediately?" the little guy asked.

"Every restaurant has been standing by for this, Mr. Carr," said the manager. "It's on its way. Prepared, of course—it's been ready since he first arrived."

"Fine," said the little guy, Carr. "It can't be too soon. He's very hungry."

I glanced around and noticed for the first time that there was nobody else in the restaurant. It was past the dinner hour, but, even so, there are always late diners. We had the place all to ourselves and it bothered me. They could have ganged up on me....

But they didn't. A light gong sounded, and the waiter and manager hurried over to a slot of a door and brought out a couple of trays loaded with covered dishes.

"Your dinner, Mr. Weldon," the manager said, putting the plates in front of me and removing the lids.

I stared down at the food.

"This," I told them angrily, "is a hell of a trick to play on a starving man!"

*

They all looked unhappy.

"Mashed dehydrated potatoes, canned meat and canned vegetables," Carr replied. "Not very appetizing. I know, but I'm afraid it's all we can allow you to eat."

I took the cover off the dessert dish.

"Dried fruits!" I said in disgust.

"Rather excessively dried, I'm sorry to say," the manager agreed mournfully.

I sipped the blue stuff in a glass and almost spat it out. "Powdered milk! Are these things what you people have to live on?"

"No, our diet is quite varied," Carr said in embarrassment. "But we unfortunately can't give you any of the foods we normally eat ourselves."

"And why in blazes not?"

"Please eat, Mr. Weldon," Carr begged with frantic earnestness. "There's so much to explain—this is part of it, of course—and it would be best if you heard it on a full stomach."

I was famished enough to get the stuff down, which wasn't easy; uninviting as it looked, it tasted still worse.

When I was through, Carr pushed several buttons on the glowing menu. Dishes came up from an opening in the center of the table and he showed me the luscious foods they contained.

"Given your choice," he said, "you'd have preferred them to what you have eaten. Isn't that so, Mr. Weldon?"

"You bet I would!" I answered, sore because I hadn't been given that choice.

"And you would have died like the pathetic old people you were investigating," said a voice behind me.

I turned around, startled. Several men and women had come in while I'd been eating, their footsteps as silent as cats on a rug. I looked blankly from them to Carr and back again.

"These are the clothes we ordinarily wear," Carr said. "An 18th Century motif, as you can see—updated knee breeches and shirt waists, a modified stock for the men, the daring low bodices of that era, the full skirts treated in a modern way by using sheer materials for the women, bright colors and sheens, buckled shoes of spun synthetics. Very gay, very ornamental, very comfortable, and thoroughly suitable to our time."

"But everybody I saw was dressed like me!" I protested.

"Only to keep you from feeling more conspicuous and anxious than you already were. It was quite a project, I can tell you—your styles varied so greatly from decade to decade, especially those for women—and the materials were a genuine problem; they'd gone out of existence long ago. We had the textile and tailoring cities working a full six months to clothe the inhabitants of this city, including, of course, the children. Everybody had to be clad as your contemporaries were, because we knew only that you would arrive in this vicinity, not where you might wander through the city."

"There was one small difference you didn't notice," added a handsome mature woman. "You were the only man in a gray suit. We had a full description of what you were wearing, you see, and we made sure nobody else was dressed that way. Naturally, everyone knew who you were, and so we were kept informed of your movements."

"What for?" I demanded in alarm. "What's this all about?"

*

Pulling up chairs, they sat down, looking to me like a witchcraft jury from some old painting.

"I'm Leo Blundell," said a tall man in plum-and-gold clothes. "As chairman of—of the Mark Weldon Committee, it's my responsibility to handle this project correctly."

"Project?"

"To make certain that history is fulfilled, I have to tell you as much as you must know."

"I wish *somebody* would!"

"Very well, let me begin by telling you much of what you undoubtedly know already. In a sense, you are more a victim of Dr. Anthony Roberts than his daughter. Roberts was a brilliant physicist, but because of his eccentric behavior, he was ridiculed for his theories and hated for his arrogance. He was an almost perfect example of self-defeat, the way in which a man will hamper his career and wreck his happiness, and then blame the world for his failure and misery. To get back to his connection with you, however, he invented a time machine—unfortunately, its secret has since been lost and never re-discovered—and used it for anti-social purposes. When he died, his daughter May carried on his work. It was she who sent you to this time to learn the principle by which the Dynapack operates. She was a thoroughly ruthless woman."

"Are you sure?" I asked uneasily.

"Quite sure."

"I know a number of old people died after she sent them on errands through time, but she said they'd lied about their age and health."

"One would expect her to say that," a woman put in cuttingly.

Blundell turned to her and shook his head. "Let Mr. Weldon clarify his feelings about her, Rhoda. They are obviously very mixed."

"They are," I admitted. "She seemed hard, the first time I saw her, when I answered her ad, but she could have been just acting businesslike. I mean she had a lot of people to pick from and she had to be impersonal and make certain she had the right one. The next time—I hope you don't know about that—it was really my fault for breaking into her room. I really had a lot of admiration for the way she handled the situation."

"Go on," Carr encouraged me.

"And I can't complain about the deal she gave me. Sure, she came out ahead on the money I bet and invested for her. But I did all right myself—I was richer than I'd ever been in my life—and she gave that money to me before I even did anything to earn it!"

"Besides which," somebody else said, "she offered you half of the profits on the Dynapack."

*

I looked around at the faces for signs of hostility. I saw none. That was surprising. I'd come from the past to steal something from them and they weren't at all angry. Well, no, it wasn't really stealing. I wouldn't be depriving them of the Dynapack. It just would have been invented before it was supposed to be.

"She did," I said. "Though I wouldn't call that part of it philanthropy. She needed me for the data and I needed her to manufacture the things."

"And she was a very beautiful woman," Blundell added.

I squirmed a bit. "Yes."

"Mr. Weldon, we know a good deal about her from notes that have come down to us among her private papers. She had a safety deposit box under a false name. I won't tell you the name; it was not discovered until many years later, and we will not voluntarily meddle with the past."

I sat up and listened sharply. "So that's how you knew who I was and what I'd be wearing and what I came for! You even knew when and where I'd arrive!"

"Correct," Blundell said.

"What else do you know?"

"That you suspected her of being responsible for the deaths of many old people by starvation. Your suspicion was justified, except that her father had caused all those that occurred before 1947, when she took over after his own death. All but two people were sent into the past. Roberts was curious about the future, of course, but he did not want to waste a victim on a trip that would probably be fruitless. In the past, you understand, he knew precisely what he was after. The future was completely unknown territory."

"But she took the chance," I said.

"If you can call deliberate murder taking a chance, yes. One man arrived in 2094, over fifty years ago. The other was yourself. The first one, as you know, died of malnutrition when he was brought back to your era."

"And what happened to me?" I asked, jittering.

"You will not die. We intend to make sure of that. All the other

51

victims—I presume you're interested in their errands?"

"I think I know, but I'd like to find out just the same."

"They were sent to the past to buy or steal treasures of various sorts—art, sculpture, jewelry, fabulously valuable manuscripts and books, anything that had great scarcity value."

"That's not possible," I objected. "She had all the money she wanted. Any time she needed more, all she had to do was send somebody back to put down bets and buy stocks that she knew were winners. She had the records, didn't she? There was no way she or her father could lose!"

*

He moved his shoulders in a plum-and-gold shrug. "Most of the treasures they accumulated were for acquisition's sake—and for the sake of vengeance for the way they believed Dr. Roberts had been treated. When there were unusual expenses, such as replacing the very costly parts of the time machine, that required more than they could produce in ready cash, both Roberts and his daughter 'discovered' these treasures."

He waited while I digested the miserable meal and the disturbing information he had given me. I thought I'd found a loophole in his explanation: "You said people were sent back to the past to *buy* treasures, besides stealing them."

"I did," he agreed. "They were provided with currency of whatever era they were to visit."

I felt my forehead wrinkle up as my theory fell apart. "Then they could buy food. Why should they have died of malnutrition?"

"Because, as May Roberts herself told you, nothing can exist before it exists. Neither can anything exist after it is out of existence. If you returned with a Dynapack, for example, it would revert to a lump of various metals, because that was what it was in your period. But let me give you a more personal instance. Do you remember coming back from your first trip with dust on your hand?"

"Yes. I must have fallen."

"On one hand? No, Mr. Weldon. May Roberts was greatly upset by the incident; she was afraid you would realize why the hamburger had turned to dust—and why the old people died of starvation. *All* of them, not just a few."

He paused, giving me a chance to understand what he had just said. I did, with a sick shock.

"If I ate your food," I said shakily, "I'd feel satisfied until I was returned to my own time. *But the food wouldn't go along with me!*"

*

Blundell nodded gravely. "And so you, too, would die of malnutrition. The foods we have given you existed in your era. We were very careful of that, so careful that many of them probably were stored years before you left your time. We regret that they are not very palatable, but at least we are positive they will go back with you. You will be as healthy when you arrive in the past as when you left.

"Incidentally, she made you change your clothes for the same reason—they had been made in 1930. She had clothing from every era she wanted visited and chose old people who would fit them best. Otherwise, you see, they'd have arrived naked."

I began to shake as if I were as old as I'd pretended to be on the stage. "She's going to pull me back! If I don't bring her the information about the Dynapack, she'll shoot me!"

"That, Mr. Weldon, is our problem," Blundell said, putting his hand comfortingly on my arm to calm me.

"Your problem? I'm the one who'll get shot, not you!"

"But we know in complete detail what will happen when you are returned to the 20th Century."

I pulled my arm away and grabbed his. "You know that? Tell me!"

"I'm sorry, Mr. Weldon. If we tell you what you did, you might think of some alternate action, and there is no knowing what the result would be."

"But I didn't get shot or die of malnutrition?"

"That much we can tell you. Neither."

They all stood up, so bright and attractive in their colorful clothes that I felt like a shirt-sleeved stage hand who'd wandered in on a costume play.

"You will be returned in a month, according to the notes May Roberts left. She gave you plenty of time to get the data, you see. We propose to make that month an enjoyable one for you. The resources of our city—and any others you care to visit—are at your disposal. We wish you to take full advantage of them."

"And the Dynapack?"

"Let us worry about that. We want you to have a good time while you are our guest."

I did.

It was the most wonderful month of my life.

*

The mesh cage blurred around me. I could see May Roberts through it, her hand just leaving the switch. She was as beautiful as ever, but I saw beneath her beauty the vengeful, vicious creature her father's bitterness had turned her into; Blundell and Carr had let me read some of her notes, and I knew. I wished I could have spent the rest of my years in the future, instead of having to come back to this.

She came over and opened the gate, smiling like an angel welcoming a bright new soul. Then her eyes traveled startledly over me and her smile almost dropped off. But she held it firmly in place.

She had to, while she asked, "Do you have the notes I sent you for?"

"Right here," I said.

I reached into my breast pocket and brought out a stubby automatic and shot her through the right arm. Her closed hand opened and a little derringer clanked on the floor. She gaped at me with an expression of horrified surprise that should have been recorded permanently; it would have served as a model for generations of actors and actresses.

"You—brought back a weapon!" she gasped. "You shot me!" She

stared vacantly at her bleeding arm and then at my automatic. "But you can't—bring anything back from the future. And you aren't—dying of malnutrition."

She said it all in a voice shocked into toneless wonder.

"The food I ate and this gun are from the present," I said. "The people of the future knew I was coming. They gave me food that wouldn't vanish from my cells when I returned. They also gave me the gun instead of the plans for the Dynapack."

"And you took it?" she screamed at me. "You idiot! I'd have shared the profits honestly with you. You'd have been worth millions!"

"With acute malnutrition," I amended. "I like it better this way, thanks—poor, but alive. Or relatively poor, I should say, because you've been very generous and I appreciate it."

"By shooting me!"

"I hated to puncture that lovely arm, but it wasn't as painful as starving or getting shot myself. Now if you don't mind—or even if you do—it's your turn to get into the cage, Miss Roberts."

She tried to grab for the derringer on the floor with her left hand.

"Don't bother," I said quietly. "You can't reach it before a bullet reaches you."

*

She straightened up, staring at me for the first time with terror in her eyes.

"What are you going to do to me?" she whispered.

"I could kill you as easily as you could have killed me. Kill you and send your body into some other era. How many dozens of deaths were you responsible for? The law couldn't convict you of them, but I can. And I couldn't be convicted, either."

She put her hand on the wound. Blood seeped through her fingers as she lifted her chin at me.

"I won't beg for my life, Weldon, if that's what you want. I could offer you a partnership, but I'm not really in a position to offer it, am I?"

She was magnificent, terrifyingly intelligent, brave clear through ... and deadlier than a plague. I had to remember that.

"Into the cage," I said. "I have some friends in the future who have plans for you. I won't tell you what they are, of course; you didn't tell me what I'd go through, did you? Give my friends my fondest regards. If I can manage it, I'll visit them—and you."

She backed warily into the cage. It would have been pleasant to kiss those wonderful lips good-by. I'd thought about them for a whole month, wanting them and loathing them at the same time.

It would have been like kissing a coral snake. I knew it and I concentrated on shutting the gate on her.

"You'd like to be rich, wouldn't you, Weldon?" she asked through the mesh.

"I can be," I said. "I have the machine. I can send people into the past or future and make myself a pile of dough. Only I'd give them food to take along. I wouldn't kill them off to keep the secret to myself. Anything else on your mind?"

"You want me," she stated.

I didn't argue.

"You could have me."

"Just long enough to get my throat slit or brains blown out. I don't want anything that much."

I rammed the switch closed.

The mesh cage blurred and she was gone. Her blood was on the floor, but she was gone into the future I had just come from.

That was when the reaction hit me. I'd escaped starvation and her gun, but I wasn't a hero and the release of tension flipped my stomach over and unhinged my knees.

Shaking badly, I stumbled through the big, empty house until I found a phone.

*

Lou Pape got there so quickly that I still hadn't gotten over the tremors, in spite of a bottle of brandy I dug out of a credenza, maybe because the date on the label, 1763, gave me a new case of the shivers.

I could see the worry on Lou's face vanish when he assured himself that I was all right. It came back again, though, when I told him what had happened. He didn't believe any of it, naturally. I guess I hadn't really expected him to.

"If I didn't know you, Mark," he said, shaking his big, dark head unhappily, "I'd send you over to Bellevue for observation. Even knowing you, maybe that's what I ought to do."

"All right, let's see if there's any proof," I suggested tiredly. "From what I was told, there ought to be plenty."

We searched the house clear down to the basement, where he stood with his face slack.

"Christ!" he breathed. "The annex to the Metropolitan Museum!"

The basement ran the length and breadth of the house and was twice as high as an average room, and the whole glittering place was crammed with paintings in rich, heavy frames, statuettes, books, manuscripts, goblets and ewers and jewelry made of gold and huge gems, and tapestries in brilliant color ... and everything was as bright and sparkling and new as the day it was made, which was almost true of a lot of it.

"The dame was loaded and she was an art collector, that's all," Lou said. "You can't sell me that screwy story of yours. She was a collector and she knew where to find things."

"She certainly did," I agreed.

"What did you do with her?"

"I told you. I shot her through the arm before she could shoot me and I sent her into the future."

He took me by the front of the jacket. "You killed her, Mark. You wanted all this stuff for yourself, so you knocked her off and got rid of her body somehow."

"Why don't you go back to acting, where you belong, Lou, and leave sleuthing to people who know how?" I asked, too worn to pull his hands loose. "Would I kill her and call you up to get right over here? Wouldn't I have sneaked these things out first? Or more likely I'd have sneaked them out, hidden them and nobody—including you—would know I'd ever been here. Come on, use your head."

"That's easy. You lost your nerve."

"I'm not even losing my patience."

*

He pushed me away savagely. "If you killed her for this stuff or because of that crazy yarn you gave me, I'm a cop and you're no friend. You're just a plain killer I happened to have known once, and I'll make sure you fry."

"You always did have a taste for that kind of dialogue. Go ahead and wrap me up in an airtight case, have them throw the book at me, send me up the river, put me in the hot squat. But you'll have to do the proving, not me."

He headed for the stairs. "I will. And don't try to make a break or I'll plug you as if I never saw you before."

He put in a call at the phone upstairs. I didn't give a particular damn who it was he'd called. I was too relieved that I hadn't killed May Roberts; destroying anything that beautiful, however evil, would have stayed with me the rest of my life. There was another reason for my relief—if I'd killed her and left the evidence for Lou to find, he'd never help me. No, that's not quite so; he'd probably have tried to get me to plead insanity on the basis of my unbelievable explanation.

But most of all, I couldn't get rid of the look on her face when I'd shot her through the arm, the arm that was so wonderful to look at and that had held a murderous little gun to greet me with.

She was in the future now. She wouldn't be executed by them; they regarded crime as an illness, and they'd treat her with their marvelously advanced therapy and she'd become a useful, contented citizen, living out her existence in an era that had given me more happiness than I'd ever had.

I sat and tried to stupefy myself with brandy that should long ago have dried to brick-hardness, while Lou Pape stood at the door with his hand near his holster and glared at me. He didn't take his eyes off me until somebody named Prof. Jeremiah Aaronson came in and was introduced briefly and flatly to me. Then Lou took him upstairs.

It was minutes before I realized what they were going to do. I ran up after them.

I was just in time to see Aaronson carefully take the housing off the hooded motors, and leap back suddenly from the fury of lightning sparks.

*

The whole machine fused while we watched helplessly—motors, switches, panel and mesh cage. They flashed blindingly and blew apart and melted together in a charred and molten pile.

"Rigged," Aaronson said in the tone of a bitter curse. "Set to short if it was tampered with. I wouldn't be surprised if there were incendiaries placed at strategic spots. Nothing else could have made a mess like this."

He finally glanced down at his hand and saw it was scorched. He hissed with the realization of pain, blew on the burn, shook it in the air to cool it, and pulled a handkerchief out of his back pocket by reaching all the way around the rear for it with his left hand.

Lou looked helplessly at the heap of cooling slag. "Can you make any sense of it, Prof?" he asked.

"Can you?" Aaronson retorted. "Melt down a microtome or any other piece of machinery you're unfamiliar with, and see if you can identify it when it looks like this."

He went out, wrapping his hand in the handkerchief.

Lou kicked glumly at a piece of twisted tubing. "Aaronson is a top physicist, Mark. I was hoping he'd make enough out of the machine to—ah, hell, I wanted to believe you! I couldn't. I still can't. Now we'll have to dig through the house to find her body."

"You won't find it or the secret of the machine," I answered miserably. "I told you they said the secret would be lost. This is how. Now I'll never be able to visit the future again. I'll never see them or May Roberts. They'll straighten her out, get rid of her hate and vindictiveness, and it won't do me a damned bit of good because the machine is gone and she's generations ahead of me."

He turned to me puzzledly. "You're not afraid to have us dig for her body, Mark?"

"Tear the place apart if you want."

"We'll have to," he said. "I'm calling Homicide."

"Call in the Marines. Call in anybody you like."

"You'll have to stay in my custody until we're through."

I shrugged. "As long as you leave me alone while you're doing your digging, I don't give a hang if I'm under arrest for suspicion of murder. I've got to do some straightening out. I wish the people in the future could take on the job—they could do it faster and better than I can—but some nice, peaceful quiet would help."

*

He didn't touch me or say a word to me as we waited for the squad to arrive. I sat in the chair and shut out first him and then the men with their sounding hammers and crowbars and all the rest.

She'd been ruthless and callous, and she'd murdered old people with no more pity than a wolf among a herd of helpless sheep.

But Blundell and Carr had told me that she was as much a victim as the oldsters who'd died of starvation with the riches she'd given them still untouched, on deposit in the banks or stuffed into hiding places or pinned to their shabby clothes. She needed treatment for the illness her father had inflicted on her. But even he, they'd said, had been suffering from a severe emotional disturbance and proper care could have made a great and honored scientist out of him.

They'd told me the truth and made me hate her, and they'd told me their viewpoint and made that hatred impossible.

I was here, in the present, without her. The machine was gone.

Yearning over something I couldn't change would destroy me. I had no right to destroy myself. Nobody did, they'd told me, and nobody who reconciles himself to the fact that some situations just are impossible to work out ever could.

I'd realized that when the squad packed up and left and Lou Pape came over to where I was sitting.

"You knew we wouldn't find her," he said.

"That's what I kept telling you."

"Where is she?"

"In Port Said, exotic hellhole of the world, where she's dancing in veils for the depraved—"

"Cut out the kidding! Where is she?"

"What's the difference, Lou? She's not here, is she?"

"That doesn't mean she can't be somewhere else, dead."

"She's not dead. You don't have to believe me about anything else, just that."

He hauled me out of the chair and stared hard at my face. "You aren't lying," he said. "I know you well enough to know you're not."

"All right, then."

"But you're a damned fool to think a dish like that would have any part of you. I don't mean you're nothing a woman would go for, but she's more fang than female. You'd have to be richer and better-looking than her, for one thing—"

"Not after my friends get through with her. She'll know a good man when she sees one and I'd be what she wants." I slid my hand over my naked scalp. "With a head of hair, I'd look my real age, which happens to be a year younger than you, if you remember. She'd go for me—they checked our emotional quotients and we'd be a natural together. The only thing was that I was bald. They could have grown hair on my head, which would have taken care of that, and then we'd have gotten together like gin and tonic."

*

Lou arched his black eyebrows at me. "They really could grow hair on you?"

"Sure. Now you want to know why I didn't let them." I glanced out the window at the smoky city. "That's why. They couldn't tell me if I'd ever get back to the future. I wasn't taking any chances. As long as there was a possibility that I'd be stranded in my own time, I wasn't going to lose my livelihood. Which reminds me, you have anything else to do here?"

"There'll be a guard stationed around the house and all her holdings and art will be taken over until she comes back—"

"She won't."

"—or is declared legally dead."

"And me?" I broke in.

"We can't hold you without proof of murder."

"Good enough. Then let's get out of here."

"I have to go back on duty," he objected.

"Not any more. I've got over $15,000 in cash and deposits—enough to finance you and me."

"Enough to kill her for."

"Enough to finance you and me," I repeated doggedly. "I told you I had the money before she sent me into the future—"

"All right, all right," he interrupted. "Let's not go into that again. We couldn't find a body, so you're free. Now what's this about financing the two of us?"

I put my fingers around his arm and steered him out to the street.

"This city has never had a worse cop than you," I said. "Why? Because you're an actor, not a cop. You're going back to acting, Lou. This money will keep us both going until we get a break."

He gave me the slit-eyed look he'd picked up in line of duty. "That wouldn't be a bribe, would it?"

"Call it a kind of memorial to a lot of poor, innocent old people and a sick, tormented woman."

We walked along in silence out in the clean sunshine. It was our silence; the sleek cars and burly trucks made their noise and the pedestrians added their gabble, but a good Stanislavsky actor like Lou wouldn't notice that. Neither would I, ordinarily, but I was giving him a chance to work his way through this situation.

"I won't hand you a lie, Mark," he said finally. "I never stopped wanting to act. I'll take your deal on two considerations."

"All right, what are they?"

"That whatever I take off you is strictly a loan."

"No argument. What's the other?"

He had an unlit cigarette almost to his lips. He held it there while he said: "That any time you come across a case of an old person who died of starvation with $30,000 stashed away somewhere, you turn fast to the theatrical page and not tell me or even think about it."

"I don't have to agree to that."

*

He lowered the cigarette, stopped and turned to me. "You mean it's no deal?"

"Not that," I said. "I mean there won't be any more of those cases. Between knowing that and both of us back acting again, I'm satisfied. You don't have to believe me. Nobody does."

He lit up and blew out a pretty plume, fine and slow and straight, which would have televised like a million in the bank. Then he grinned. "You wouldn't want to bet on that, would you?"

"Not with a friend. I do all my sure-thing betting with bookies."

"Then make it a token bet," he said. "One buck that somebody dies of starvation with a big poke within a year."

I took the bet.

I took the dollar a year later.

www.ingramcontent.com/pod-product-compliance
Lightning Source LLC
Chambersburg PA
CBHW020342130626
46549CB00003B/1249